You're My Nikki

by **Phyllis Rose Eisenberg** / *pictures by* **Jill Kastner**

DIAL BOOKS FOR YOUNG READERS NEW YORK

Published by Dial Books for Young Readers
A Division of Penguin Books USA Inc.
375 Hudson Street
New York, New York 10014

Designed by Nancy R. Leo
Printed in the U.S.A.
First Edition
1 3 5 7 9 10 8 6 4 2

Library of Congress Cataloging in Publication Data
Eisenberg, Phyllis Rose.
You're my Nikki / by Phyllis Rose Eisenberg;
pictures by Jill Kastner.
p.   cm.
Summary: Nikki needs reassurance that her mother
won't forget her when she goes out to work.
ISBN 0-8037-1127-1 (trade); ISBN 0-8037-1129-8 (lib. bdg.)
[1. Working mothers—Fiction. 2. Mothers and daughters—Fiction.]
I. Kastner, Jill, ill. II. Title.
PZ7.E3463Yo 1992   [E]—dc20   91-2670   CIP   AC

The art for this book was prepared by using oil paints.
It was then color-separated and reproduced in red, yellow, blue,
and black halftones.

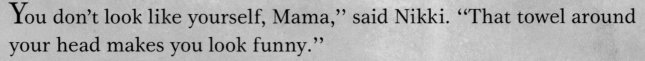

You don't look like yourself, Mama," said Nikki. "That towel around your head makes you look funny."

"I'm me," her mother laughed. "I'm the same Mama as this morning, the same Mama who just pressed her going-to-work skirt, the same Mama who just washed her hair."

"Then who am *I*, same Mama?"

"You're my Nikki. I'd know you if you were wearing two circus tents, and you sounded like a hoarse nanny goat."

"But what if you forget me at your new job tomorrow?"

Her mother shook her head. "No way! I've only got one Nikki. Now come and help me sort the laundry."

"Wait, Mama! How will you remember all my favorite things?"

"I just will. I know my girl," her mother said as she opened the hamper.

"Then what's my favorite trick?"

"A somersault."

"Now watch, Mama! I do it like this." And Nikki did three somersaults. "Did you watch?"

"With both eyes. You'll probably be a famous gymnast one day."

"Really, Mama?"

"Sure. You could even win the Gold in the Olympics, and then I'd say, 'I've known that champion since she was six pounds and one ounce. She's my Nikki!' "

"But what if my name *wasn't* Nikki?"

"Even if it was Hocus Pocus Mocus, I'd still know you."

"Even if my nose reached my chin?"

"Even if it reached your belly button."

"But *how* would you know me, Mama?"

"My heart would know."

Nikki watched as her mother put the soap in the washing machine. She was quiet for a very long time. Finally she said, "Who's my favorite friend, Mama?"

"Your favorite friend is Laurie and your favorite holiday is your birthday."

Her mother went into the kitchen. Nikki followed her. "And your favorite mama is Rena, and that's *me*."

"And blue's my best color. What's yours, Rena?"

"Red."

"Red is Michael's too," and Nikki went into her brother's bedroom and put on his pants and shoes.

When she came back to the kitchen, she said, "Who am I now, Mama?"

"You're my Nikki."

"But don't I look like Michael?"

"You do remind me of him. But I thought he was reading the Sunday comics."

"Well, he said the comics grew wings and flew away."

"Michael," said Nikki's mother, "you get the wildest ideas!"

"I'm not *really* Michael."

"I know," said her mother.

"Then what's my favorite dance?"

"How can I forget? It's 'Skip to My Lou.' You've been dancing it every day for months."

"I do it like this," said Nikki. And she danced around the room.

"You'll probably be one of the leading 'Skip to My Lou' experts of the world," said her mother.

"Really, Mama?"

"Sure. With all that practice, they'll probably write about you in a book of records….Come on, Nikki, let's finish this puzzle."

"Later," said Nikki, going into the bedroom she shared with her sister. She took her sister's blouse from the closet and a hat from the dresser. She put them on and went to show her mother.

"Who am I this time, Mama?"
Nikki's mother glanced at her from over the newspaper.
"Well, I'll be a purple giraffe. I do believe you're my Nikki!"
"But don't I look like Sharon?"
"You do remind me of her. But I thought she was practicing her piano lessons."
"Well, she threw the piano out of the window."
"Sharon," said Nikki's mother as she touched her arm, "what muscles! Have you been working overtime on your weight lifting?"

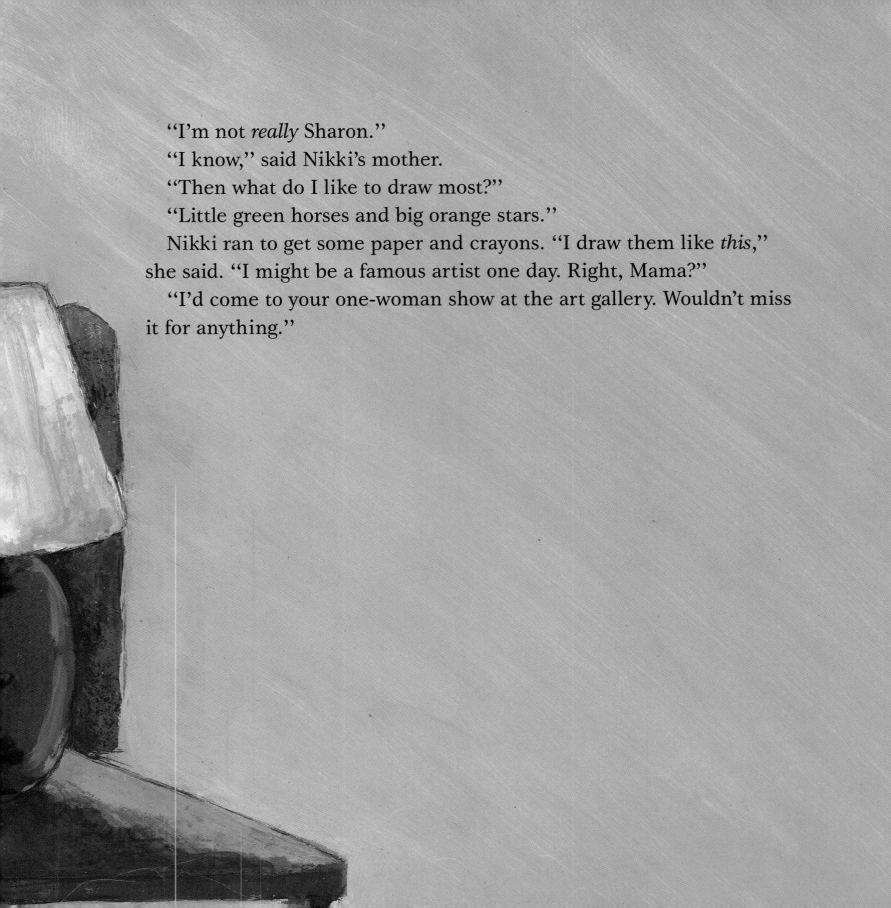

"I'm not *really* Sharon."

"I know," said Nikki's mother.

"Then what do I like to draw most?"

"Little green horses and big orange stars."

Nikki ran to get some paper and crayons. "I draw them like *this*," she said. "I might be a famous artist one day. Right, Mama?"

"I'd come to your one-woman show at the art gallery. Wouldn't miss it for anything."

Nikki pulled a chair close to her mother. "My favorite rainy day thing is jumping over puddles," she said. "And butterscotch pudding's my favorite dessert. What're your favorites, Mama?"

"Now let me think....For rainy days I love reading in the bathtub best. And for dessert—I know! Pecan pie!"

"I don't like pecan pie....Mama, what if I forget *you*?"

"I'll be home before dinner, honey," said Nikki's mother, squeezing her hand. "We'll know each other."

The next day when her mother came home from her new job, Nikki said, "Who am I, Mama?"

"Nikki," said her mother, and then called, "Sharon, please help with the groceries! And set the table, Michael!"

"But why didn't you say, 'You're my Nikki'?"

"I'm very tired. Please wash your hands and get the milk and bread."

"But I'm wearing your old glasses. Don't I look different?"

"A little," said Nikki's mother. "Don't forget the napkins, Michael!"

"I don't think you know me, Mama," said Nikki.

"I do. Now wash and help with dinner."

"Then what's my favorite sport?" said Nikki, setting the milk on the table.

"Jumping rope."

"No, it isn't!"

"Sharon," called Nikki's mother, "please stir the rice!"

"But jumping rope is wrong!" said Nikki.

"Michael," called Nikki's mother, "turn down that stereo!"

"I knew you'd forget me," said Nikki softly. And she was very quiet at dinner.

Later, when her mother came to tuck her in, Nikki hid under the
covers.

"Where's my Nikki?" said her mother.

Nikki didn't answer.

"Are *you* my Nikki?" asked her mother, gently shaking her.

"Not anymore," said Nikki.

"I wish you were," her mother said sadly.

"You don't even know her!" said Nikki, poking her head out. "You don't even care! You probably think she likes to draw *rats* and that she doesn't do *anything* on rainy days!"

"No!" said her mother. "My Nikki likes to draw horses and stars. And she jumps over rain puddles! And she loves butterscotch pudding. And her birthday. And somersaults. Isn't that right?"

Nikki held her teddy bear tightly. She didn't answer her mother.

"And she loves Laurie. And blue. And she 'Skips to My Lou' like this." Nikki's mother started to dance.

"Not like *that*!" said Nikki, getting out of bed. "Like *this*!"

"And bike riding is her favorite sport."

"Jumping rope *used* to be," said Nikki. "You forgot, and you forgot me too."

"It only seemed that way, honey. I was busy and tired, but I can't really forget you—ever."

"Well...," said Nikki, "I think *I* forgot *you*!"

"I hope not," said her mother, sitting on Nikki's bed. "What's my favorite color and rainy day thing and dessert?"

"…gray," said Nikki softly. "…watching TV…graham crackers."

"No! Red! Reading in the bathtub! Pecan pie!"

"Mama," said Nikki, "I didn't really forget you."

"I know," said her mother.

"We'll never forget each other," said Nikki. "Even when you come home from your new job."

Nikki's mother sighed. "I didn't like my job today. There's so much to remember."

"But maybe tomorrow you will. And by the next day you could even be famous for remembering. And I'll say, 'She's Rena, my mama. I've known her forever.' "

"I'm the gladdest Mama in the world," said Nikki's mother as she hugged her, "and it's because—"

"I'm your Nikki," said Nikki, smiling.